Supernova!

Story by Heather Hammonds

Illustrations by Lisa Simmons

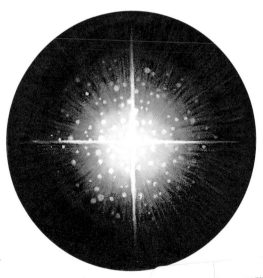

PM Chapter Books
part of the Rigby PM Collection

U.S. edition © 2001 Rigby
a division of Reed Elsevier Inc.
500 Coventry Lane
Crystal Lake, IL 60014
www.rigby.com

Text © 2001 Nelson Thomson Learning
Illustrations © 2001 Nelson Thomson Learning
Originally published in Australia by Nelson Thomson Learning

06 05 04 03 02 01
10 9 8 7 6 5 4 3 2 1

Supernova!
ISBN 0 7635 7791 X

Printed in China by Midas Printing (Asia) Ltd

Contents

Chapter 1

Ready to Go

Amy looked out of her bedroom window and saw the moon and the stars shining brightly in the sky.

"Time to go," she said to herself.

She ran down to the garage and carefully wheeled out the large telescope that her father had given her for her birthday. Amy's father was an astronomer and he had built the telescope himself. It was called a Newtonian reflecting telescope. When Amy used it, she looked through a little tube in its side called an eyepiece.

Amy wheeled the telescope right into the middle of her backyard. Then she went back into the garage and brought out two folding chairs. She was almost ready for action. She put her fingers to her mouth and whistled. After a few minutes she heard a sound.

"Are you there, Amy?" whispered James, climbing up the fence that separated their yards.

"Yes," she called softly. "Hurry up. It's time to go!"

James had moved next door to Amy a few weeks before, and he and Amy had become good friends. Every night when the sky was clear, they could be found outside, looking through the telescope at the moon, the stars, and the planets.

James jumped down into Amy's yard and ran over to her. Amy made some last-minute changes to the telescope.

"Okay," she said. "It's ready."

Chapter 2

Moon Flight

Amy swung her telescope around and pointed it at the moon. The moon was so big and bright tonight. She imagined she was flying over it in a spaceship. She saw mountains and valleys, hundreds of craters, and the dark, gray "seas," or "maria," as her father called them.

Amy wanted to be an astronaut when she got older, so that she could really fly a spaceship to the moon.

"Can I take over now?" asked James.

Amy moved over and let James take a turn. He loved looking through her telescope, and wanted to be an astronaut one day, too. He dreamed of traveling to different planets and stars, and maybe even discovering new worlds.

"We're flying over the Sea of Tranquility," he said, turning the telescope around a little bit. "It looks pretty good down there tonight."

James was just about to let Amy have another look, when the light of four flashlights suddenly shone on them.

"Hey, everyone, it's Space Woman," said a voice. "Look at her! She thinks she's on a spaceship or something."

James and Amy looked toward the voice. There were four shadows sitting on the fence.

"Go away, Tony," sighed Amy.

Tony lived on the other side of Amy's house, and he and his three friends went to Amy's school. They thought that she was strange because she was interested in astronomy.

"Space Woman has a boyfriend," snickered Tony, shining his flashlight on James. "He's just as weird as she is!"

Tony's friends laughed and waved their flashlights around.

"Space Woman's got a boyfriend," they chanted.

"Don't pay any attention," said James.

He and Amy tried to ignore Tony and his friends. After a while, Tony got tired of teasing them and they all went away.

"Next time, why don't you bring your telescope over to my house?" said James. "My parents won't mind, and Tony and his miserable friends won't be able to bother us."

Amy nodded, feeling angry that they had been laughed at and called names. It had spoiled their fun.

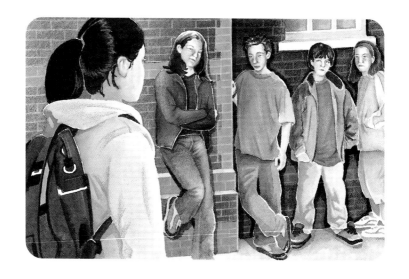

Tony and his friends were waiting for Amy when she arrived at school the next morning.

"Where's your boyfriend, Space Woman?" asked Tony.

"James doesn't go to this school," mumbled Amy. "And he's not my boyfriend!"

"Yes, he is," laughed one of the girls. "You were kissing him!"

"I was not!" hissed Amy, her face getting red.

The other children in the school yard stared at Amy as Tony and his friends kept teasing her.

"Amy's got a boyfriend who likes weird stuff, too."

Amy wished the school bell would ring so she could go into her classroom and get away from them.

Chapter 3
- - - - - - - - - - - - - -
Something in the Sky

That night, Amy quietly wheeled her telescope down the driveway and over to James's backyard. James was waiting for her to arrive. His mom had given him a big bag of corn chips in case they got hungry.

"Did Tony and his friends see you come over here?" asked James.

"No," replied Amy. "They won't be able to call us names tonight, but I'm sick of them teasing me. I wish I could think of a way to stop them."

"Don't worry about them," said James. "We've got more exciting things to think about."

Amy and James began to look through the telescope at the moon. They looked at some of its larger craters, trying to remember their names.

Suddenly, Amy saw a very bright star, right next to the moon. She took her eye away from the telescope and stared up into the sky, checking the star patterns around it.

"Take a look at this!" she exclaimed. "I don't think it's an ordinary star!"

James looked through the telescope.

"I'm sure it wasn't there last night," he said. "What do you think it is?"

"It might not be a star at all," said Amy. "I'm going home to get some of my astronomy books. They've got maps in them that tell you where each star in the sky should be. They're called star charts. I'll ask my dad to come and take a look, too."

While Amy ran back to her house, James kept watch through the telescope. Secretly, he felt rather scared. What could the "star" be? Surely not an alien spaceship! He and Amy sometimes pretended to be searching for alien ships when they were using the telescope, but there really were no such things ... were there?

"I'm being silly," James muttered nervously, as he sat by himself in the dark. "Just because we don't know what it is doesn't mean it has anything to do with aliens."

Chapter 4

The Exploding Star

Amy and her father hurried into James's yard, carrying books and star charts. James's parents came outside to see what was happening.

Amy looked through the telescope again and showed her father what she and James had found. They carefully checked their star charts and Amy's father, who was a very good astronomer, began to smile.

"I think it might be a supernova," he said slowly.

"What's a supernova?" asked James, feeling glad that Amy's father didn't think it was an alien ship.

"A supernova is a star that has exploded," explained Amy. "It shines very brightly when it explodes, and that's why we can see it now. It's a very long way away from us. If we had looked at that part of the sky with the telescope before it exploded, we might have seen only a tiny little star, or maybe nothing at all."

"Will our sun ever become a supernova?" asked James.

"Don't worry," smiled Amy. "Our sun is much too small to become a supernova. It usually happens to much bigger stars, or to one of a pair of stars that are very close together."

James thought about what he had been told, while Amy and her father kept looking through the telescope.

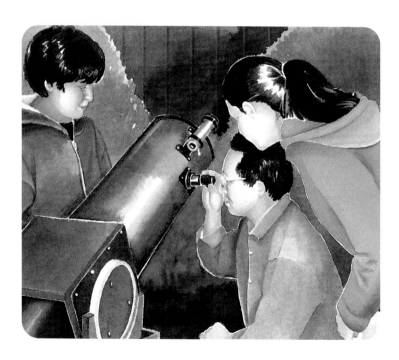

"This is amazing," said Amy. "I wonder if the supernova will get any brighter?"

"I don't know," replied Amy's father. "But you kids might have been the first to see it. We should report it to a place called the Central Bureau for Astronomical Telegrams. It collects information on supernovas from all over the world, as well as other interesting things such as comets and asteroids."

Amy's father hurried home to make the telephone call.

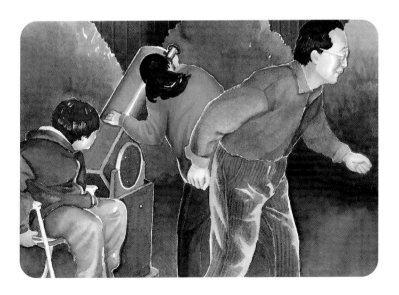

Chapter 5

A Discovery

"What happens if we did see the supernova before anyone else did?" asked James.

"We'll go down in history as its discoverers," said Amy.

The two friends stared through the telescope at the bright star until Amy's father returned.

"I've spoken to an astronomer at the bureau," he said. "It's definitely a very big supernova, and it looks as though you two really were the first to see it."

"We'll be famous," shouted James. "Will the supernova be named after us?"

"I'm afraid not," said Amy's father. "It will be given a number and letter, like all other supernovas. Something like SN 2000 A. SN stands for supernova, of course. The numbers are for the year of discovery, and the letters at the end depend on how many supernovas have already been discovered in that year."

"Oh well, at least we will always be able to look at the supernova and know that we were the ones who found it," said James.

"Don't count on it," said Amy, shaking her head. "After a while it will grow dimmer, and then we might not be able to see it anymore."

James felt sad. He wished that their exploding star could shine brightly forever.

Since the next day was a school day, Amy and James had to pack up the telescope and go inside to bed.

"Even famous astronomers need their sleep," laughed Amy's father, when they said that they wanted to stay up all night.

Just before she went to bed, Amy looked out of her window at the starry sky and thought about Tony and his friends. Suddenly she wasn't angry at them anymore. They might think that she and James were weird, but they hadn't discovered their very own supernova!

Chapter 6

An Exciting Day

The next day, Amy was awakened by a very early knock on the front door. When she opened it, she saw a group of reporters standing outside.

"Are you one of the kids who discovered the exploding star?" asked a reporter. "We would like to take a picture of you and your friend with your telescope."

"I'll run next door and get James," said Amy.

Soon Amy was standing with James in her front yard, next to the telescope. Some television people were filming them for the news, and photographers were taking their pictures for the newspapers.

"We were looking at the moon when Amy noticed the supernova right next to it," said James. "We weren't sure what it was at first, but we knew that there wasn't a bright star there the night before."

Amy saw Tony staring at them over the fence as they spoke to all the reporters. He looked very surprised.

At school that day, the principal asked Amy to give a talk on astronomy. Afterward, everyone asked her questions about the supernova. Even Tony and his friends listened carefully to everything she said.

At lunchtime, Tony came up to Amy. He looked at his feet, not at Amy.

"Um … well," he muttered. "We're sorry we made fun of you. We didn't know how exciting astronomy could be. Do you think my friends and I could come over one night and look through your telescope at your supernova?"

"Well, I suppose so," said Amy. "As long as you promise not to tease me anymore."

Chapter 7

Fame!

When Amy got home from school, her mother gave her the afternoon newspaper. There was a big picture of her with James and the telescope on the front page.

YOUNG ASTRONOMERS DISCOVER BRIGHT SUPERNOVA!

When the evening news came on, their supernova was the first story. Amy could hardly believe her eyes when she saw herself on television.

"Wow," she said. "We really ARE famous."

That night after dinner, Amy and James met in Amy's backyard again, so they could look at their supernova.

"Tony and his friends might be coming over to look through the telescope later," said Amy. She explained what had happened at lunchtime.

"That's great," said James. "We won't have to worry about them anymore."

The two friends stared up at the dark night sky.

"It was exciting seeing ourselves on television and in the papers, but I don't think it was as exciting as discovering the supernova," said Amy.

"I don't either," said James.

"But even if we never discover another supernova, it doesn't really matter," Amy went on. "We'll still be able to look at lots of fantastic things, even if we aren't the first people to see them—galaxies, stars, planets, moons."

"Well, are you ready?" asked James.

"Let's go!" grinned Amy, pointing her telescope to the sky.